The Brothers Grimm

Rapunzel

and other fairy tales

Miles Kelly

First published in 2015 by Miles Kelly Publishing Ltd
Harding's Barn, Bardfield End Green, Thaxted, Essex, CM6 3PX, UK

2 4 6 8 10 9 7 5 3 1

Publishing Director Belinda Gallagher
Creative Director Jo Cowan
Editorial Director Rosie Neave
Designer Rob Hale
Production Manager Elizabeth Collins
Reprographics Stephan Davis, Jennifer Cozens, Thom Allaway

ISBN 978-1-78209-745-7

Printed in China

British Library Cataloguing-in-Publication Data
A catalogue record for this book is available from the British Library

ACKNOWLEDGEMENTS
The publishers would like to thank the following artists who have contributed to this book:

Front cover and all border illustrations: Louise Ellis (The Bright Agency)

Inside illustrations:
Rapunzel Ayesha Lopez (Advocate-art)
The Gnome Bruno Robert (Plum Pudding Illustration Agency)
The Old Woman in the Wood Kristina Swarner (The Bright Agency)
The Lambkin and the Little Fish Martina Peluso (Advocate-art)

Made with paper from a sustainable forest

www.mileskelly.net
info@mileskelly.net

Contents

Rapunzel

Once, there lived a man and woman who were expecting their first baby. They lived in a little house which overlooked a beautiful garden, full of flowers and herbs and vegetables. However, they never dared

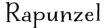

go near the garden for it did not belong to them – it belonged to a witch.

One morning, the woman was standing at her bedroom window, looking down into the witch's garden, when she saw a bed of delicious-looking salad. It looked so fresh and green that she wished with all her heart that she could eat some. Every day, her longing for the salad grew – until she found it hard to think of anything else. She became pale and miserable, and her husband began to worry that she might die. So he made up his mind to get her some.

That night, he climbed over the wall of the witch's garden, grabbed a handful of salad and hurried back to his wife. She thought it was the most delicious thing she had ever tasted. But of course it made her desperate for more…

So, the next night, her husband crept back over the wall again. To his horror, there was the witch!

"So," she hissed, pointing her bony finger at the man, "you are the one who has been stealing my salad!"

Trembling, the man explained about his sick, pregnant wife.

"Ah, I see," said the witch, softening. "In that case, take as much salad as you wish – but I have one condition… you must give me your child when it is born."

The man begged and pleaded with the

witch and offered everything else that he and his wife had, but the witch refused. The man knew the witch could do powerful magic. So he promised her what she wanted and fled back home.

Weeks passed and the man took salad for his wife every day. Then came the time when she gave birth to their child – a baby girl. The witch appeared out of thin air, picked up the child and said: "I will take good care of her." Then she disappeared…

The witch called the baby Rapunzel. She wanted Rapunzel all to herself, so she brought her up in a high tower in the middle of a huge forest, far from everything and everyone. The tower had no door or stairs, just a little

window at the top, so the witch had to magic herself in and out.

Shut away from the world, Rapunzel grew into a good, beautiful girl. By the time she was twelve, her golden hair had grown so long and thick that she could braid it and let it down out of the window like a rope, for the witch to climb up and down. But there was no way for Rapunzel herself to leave the tower.

One morning, when

Rapunzel was eighteen, a king's son was riding through the forest when he heard someone singing so sweetly that he followed the sound. It led him to the tower, for the voice was Rapunzel's. The prince rode around, trying to find a way in – but of course, there was no door. He sank down by a tree, very disappointed that he would not be able to see the singer.

While the prince sat, listening, the witch arrived. She didn't notice the prince, and strode to the bottom of the tower and cried out: "Rapunzel! Rapunzel! Let down your hair!" The golden braid came tumbling out of the window and the witch climbed up and went inside.

'Aha!' thought the prince. 'Now I see how it's done.' And he led his horse quietly away through the forest.

The prince waited till evening, then hurried back to the tower. "Rapunzel! Rapunzel! Let down your hair!" he cried, trying to sound like the witch. To his delight, the golden braid came tumbling out of the window and he climbed up and sprang inside.

Poor Rapunzel was terrified! After all, she had never seen anyone but the witch before. However, the prince spoke to her very gently and smiled so kindly that she lost her fear.

The couple talked and laughed and, before the sun rose, they had fallen in love. The prince hurried away before the witch arrived

– for she always came back in the morning – but he promised to return that very night.

And so he did… and the next night… and every night after that. Every time, the prince took with him a skein of silk – for he and Rapunzel had made a plan to run away together. She used the silk to begin weaving a long ladder. When it was ready, Rapunzel would be able to climb down from the tower too. Then the prince would whisk her away on his horse, far out of the witch's reach…

Days went by and Rapunzel's secret ladder grew longer and longer. But one day, while talking to the witch, she completely forgot herself. "You are so slow to climb – the prince is much quicker!" she exclaimed.

The witch guessed at once what was happening – and she was furious! She grabbed a pair of scissors and cut off Rapunzel's braid. Then she magicked the girl far away into an empty desert.

The witch tied Rapunzel's braid to a hook above the tower window. By and by, she heard the prince's voice calling: "Rapunzel! Rapunzel! Let down your hair," and she let the golden braid tumble to the ground.

The prince climbed up the braid – and there was the witch!

"Aha!" she cried. "Now I've got you – and you will never see Rapunzel again!" As the witch began to cast an evil spell on the prince, he leapt out of the tower window. A thick bed of thorn bushes cushioned his fall, so he was not killed – but he was seriously hurt. The sharp thorns pierced his eyes and left him blind.

To the prince, the pain of losing Rapunzel was even worse than the pain of losing his eyes. The poor young man stumbled off through the forest, broken-hearted.

And so the prince wandered over the countryside, living off nuts and berries, for more than a year – until at last he came to the desert where Rapunzel had been banished and abandoned.

The girl could not believe her eyes when she saw him. He was blind and dirty and ragged – but he was her beloved prince!

Rapunzel threw her arms around him, crying tears of joy – and as her tears fell onto the prince's eyes, they cleared. He could see once more! Finally he led Rapunzel back to his kingdom – where they lived happily ever after.

The Gnome

There was once a king who lived in a palace filled with treasures. But his favourite thing was the beautiful apple tree in his garden. Apples hung from the branches like gleaming rubies. To protect the tree the

king put a spell on it – anyone who picked an apple would sink deep underground.

One morning, the king's three daughters were walking by the apple tree when the youngest one said; "Our father loves us far too much to wish us underground – I bet the spell only works on strangers." She picked a large apple and took a bite – it was delicious! She offered it to her sisters and they tasted it too. But while they were eating, the ground became soft like sand. To their horror, they sank down and the ground closed over them.

Midday came and the three princesses did not arrive for lunch. The king ordered his servants to search everywhere in the palace and garden, but his beloved daughters were nowhere to be found. The king was beside himself with grief. He announced that whoever found his daughters and brought them back safely would have one of them as his wife.

Then all the men in the land went out into the kingdom, searching high and low.

Among them were three brothers who were huntsmen. They travelled far from their home, looking for the princesses, and reached a great castle. Strangely, the flags were flying and the drawbridge was lowered, but no one seemed to be about. The brothers entered the castle and searched the rooms, but there was not a soul to be seen.

In the great hall, the young men found the table laid with steaming plates of food. They were so hungry that they sat straight down and ate. The three tired brothers agreed that they would rest there that night, and use the castle as a base for the next few days while they continued looking for the princesses.

The following day, the eldest huntsman stayed to watch over the castle while his two younger brothers went out searching. At noon, steaming plates of food appeared on the table in the great hall once again. Then a strange little man walked in. "May I join you for lunch?" he asked.

"No you can't," said the huntsman, rudely, and he kicked the little man out.

When his brothers returned home the eldest huntsman told them all about the visit from the gnome, and what he had done.

"I'll stay and watch over the castle tomorrow," the middle brother said – and exactly the same thing happened again!

On the third day, the youngest brother stayed. All happened as before, but when the little man said, "May I join you for lunch?" the youngest brother did not refuse. Instead he replied: "Of course, be my guest."

Then the little man grinned and said: "I am a gnome and I live underground with my thousands of brothers. I can tell you where the princesses are."

He took Hans (for that was the youngest huntsman's name) and showed him a deep well. "Take a bell and a sword and go down in the bucket," the gnome instructed. "You will find three rooms below. In each one is one of the princesses with a dragon, whose many heads she has to comb. To rescue the princesses, you must cut the heads off the dragons! But beware your brothers – for they will be jealous of you and try to get rid of you." And with that, the gnome disappeared.

Hans returned to the castle and, later on, told his brothers everything – except for the gnome's warning, of course. The next morning, they went to the well together. The eldest brother said it was his right to try to rescue the princesses first. So he sat in the bucket with a bell and his sword and said, "If I ring, pull me up straight away."

The two younger brothers began to lower him down into the darkness. But the eldest huntsman became afraid before he reached the bottom, so he rang his bell and they drew him up again.

Then the second brother sat in the bucket – but he did just the same as the first.

Finally, it was Hans's turn. He sat in the

bucket all the way to the bottom. Then he jumped out, hurried to the first room, and listened outside the door. He could hear the dragon snoring loudly.

He opened the door and there was one of the princesses! She was sitting on the floor, combing the dragon's nine heads. Hans drew out his sword and hacked them off!

The princess sprang up and kissed him.

Hans went to the second princess, who had a dragon with five heads to comb, and he fought the second dragon and hacked all its heads off. At last he reached the youngest, who had a dragon with four heads, and he killed the last dragon and rescued her, too. All three princesses rejoiced and kissed him.

Then Hans sat a princess in the bucket and rang his bell very loud, and his brothers heaved her up… then the second… and then the third.

When it came to Hans's own turn, he remembered the warning of the gnome. He put a big stone in the bucket instead of himself and shouted that he was ready to be heaved up. Then his brothers began to pull and the bucket began to rise – but when it was halfway up they cut the rope and the bucket fell to the ground and was smashed to bits!

The brothers thought they had killed Hans. They made the three princesses promise not to say anything, then they took them back to the king and each demanded one of them in marriage.

Meanwhile, Hans was wondering how he would ever escape from underground. Suddenly he noticed a strange little silver flute hanging on a hook on the wall. He took it down and cautiously played a few notes on it – and all at once the room was filled with gnomes. "Why have you summoned us?" they all asked.

Hans explained that he wanted to get back above ground again, and asked politely for their help. Immediately the gnomes all took hold of him and, with one great leap, they sprang up out of the earth – and Hans was once again back in the daylight.

He hurried off at once to the king's palace and arrived not a moment too soon, for his bad brothers were just about to marry two of the princesses. All three princesses were overjoyed to see Hans, and they told the amazed king the whole story.

At once the king ordered the two wicked

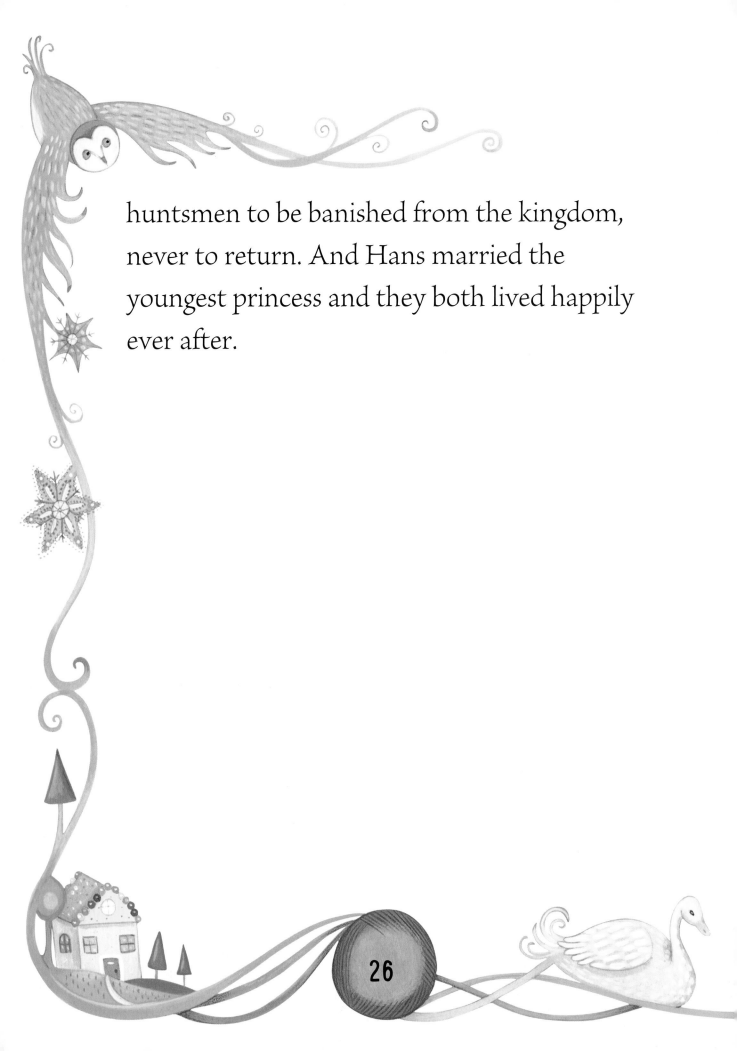

huntsmen to be banished from the kingdom, never to return. And Hans married the youngest princess and they both lived happily ever after.

The Old Woman in the Wood

There was once a poor servant girl who was sent into the forest to gather herbs. But she wandered off the path and became lost. She began to weep bitterly, crying, "What will become of me?"

She walked about and looked for the road, but could not find it. When evening drew in, she sank down under a tree, exhausted.

Then to her surprise, a white dove came flying up to her – and it had a little golden key in its beak! It put the little key in her hand, and said, "Go to that big tree over there and you will see a tiny lock in the trunk. You can open it with this key."

So the girl went to the tree and opened it. Inside was bread and cheese and milk!

The girl ate and drank and felt much better. "Now is about the time when the hens at home go into the henhouse to roost," she sighed to herself. "I wish I could get into my little bed too."

At that moment the white dove came flying up to her again, this time carrying a second little golden key in its beak. "This key will open that even bigger tree, over there," the dove instructed.

The girl opened the tree and found a beautiful little white bed inside! She couldn't believe her eyes. The girl climbed in under the soft blankets and just had time to murmer, "Oh thank you, thank you," before she fell fast asleep.

In the morning, the white dove came flying up to her for a third time. Again it brought another little gold key and told the girl to open a third tree with it. When she did so, she found beautiful clothes hanging within. They were embroidered with gold and jewels, fit for a princess.

Now the girl was much cheered up and her heart was full of hope.

"Will you do something for me?" asked the little dove.

"Of course," said the girl at once. "I would love to pay you back somehow for all the kindness you have shown me."

"Thank you," said the dove. "I will lead you to a small house. The woman who lives there will answer the door – don't speak a word to her, just go in, passing her on the right side.

"Inside the house there is a little door – open it and you will find yourself in a room filled with rings of all shapes and sizes. They will gleam and glitter with gold and silver and jewels – but you mustn't take them. Find the plainest, dullest one and bring it here to me."

The girl hurried after the dove to the little house at once. She knocked at the door and an old woman answered it. Black magic crackled and fizzed all around her, and the girl realized at once that she was a witch, and she felt afraid.

"Good day, my child," said the witch, "how can I help you?"

But the girl remembered what the dove had said and she didn't speak a word in reply. Instead, she did as the dove had asked and pushed past the witch on her right side, and though the old crone tried to grab her the girl managed to slip through her grasp.

She hurried on to the little door and went into the room filled with rings, just as the dove had described. The dazzle of the gold and silver and jewels gleamed like a rainbow in sunshine! The girl began turning them over and over, hunting for the plain, dull one – but she could not find it.

While the girl was searching, she noticed a

movement behind her. She spun round and saw that the witch was creeping out of the cottage, carrying a basket in her hand. The girl raced to the witch and seized the basket out of her crabby old hands. Inside was a little kitten which wore a ribbon round its neck. On the ribbon was a very plain, dull ring.

Quick as a flash, the girl untied the ribbon, took the ring and ran off, out of the house and back into the forest.

She didn't stop running until she was far away from the witch's house. Then she leaned against a tree to get her breath back and waited for the little white dove. She waited and waited – but he didn't come.

Just as the girl was about to despair she

suddenly felt the branches of the tree behind her move. As they wrapped around her waist they became two arms! The girl turned to find that the tree had become a handsome young man! He kissed her and said:

34

"That old witch had enchanted me: she put me under a spell where I was a dove for two hours a day and a tree for the rest of the time. By taking her ring you have broken her powers and set me free!"

As the girl smiled with delight, all the trees round about melted and changed into the young man's servants and horses – for they had been enchanted too. Then the young man led them all back to his palace – because he was a prince – where he married the brave, kind servant girl and they lived happily ever after.

The Lambkin and the Little Fish

Long ago and far away, there was a rich nobleman who lived in a big castle. His wife had died, leaving him with their two children: a little boy and a little girl. They were good children, who loved each

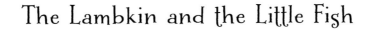

other dearly. But after a few years the nobleman married again. His new wife wasn't sweet and kind and caring like the children's mother. She was miserable and cruel and spiteful – and she was a witch!

One day, the children were playing merrily in the courtyard, in the sunshine. The witch stood watching them with hard eyes. Their laughter made her angry.

Suddenly, she muttered words of magic… *Pfff!* The little boy turned into a fish! The witch picked him up by the tail and tossed him into the castle moat. Then… *Pfff!* The witch turned the little girl into a lamb and chased her away into the

37

meadow. The evil woman turned on her heel and strode indoors, very pleased with her work. And before the day was out she cast a spell over her husband so he did not even notice that his two children were missing.

The next day, friends of the witch arrived at the castle. The witch smiled a wicked smile to herself and told the cook: "Fetch that lamb from the meadow and roast it for dinner."

So the cook went to the meadow and caught the lamb. He was outside the kitchen door, sharpening his knife, about to kill it, when he noticed a little fish swimming in the moat. To his amazement, the little lamb cried out: "Oh my brother, I will always love you!"

And the little fish called back: "Oh my sister, my heart is breaking!"

The cook was astonished. He realized that the creatures must be the missing children, under an evil spell. He stroked the lamb and whispered, "Don't worry, I won't kill you."

He scooped the fish out of the moat in a bucket of water and hid both the bucket and the lamb in the stable. He bought some meat from the butcher's to serve to the witch and her visitors – and the cruel woman never guessed the difference!

That night the kind cook took the lamb and the bucket into the forest, to a wise woman who lived there in a little cottage. Luckily, the woman knew how to undo the spell – and the little girl and little boy were soon back to their usual selves.

Of course, they could never return to the castle, so they lived with the wise woman in the forest. She taught them good magic, not black magic – and very happy the children were too.